Tickety-Tock,
WHAT TIME IS IT?

Written and illustrated
by Julie Durrell

A GOLDEN BOOK • NEW YORK

Western Publishing Company, Inc., Racine, Wisconsin 53404

Library of Congress Catalog Card Number: 88-81489 ISBN: 0-307-00308-6   MCMXCI

8:00

The clock says tickety-tock, it's eight o'clock in the morning. "Time to get up," calls Mother. "We have a busy day ahead."

First I dress, then I comb my hair and brush my teeth. I remember to make my bed and wave good-bye to teddy bear and mouse.

9:00

The clock says tickety-tock, now it's nine
o'clock. "Breakfast is ready," says Mother.
I love fresh orange juice and blueberry
pancakes with maple syrup.

10:00

The clock says tickety-tock, now it's ten o'clock. "We'd better head downtown to shop if we want to get everything you need for school tomorrow," says Mother.

I hop into the car, fasten my seat belt, and lock my door. Mother starts the engine and off we go.

11:00

The clock says tickety-tock, now it's eleven o'clock. "Since we couldn't find anything at the first shoe store, let's try the next one," suggests Mother.

I pick out sneakers in my favorite color— green! Mother also buys me loafers.

The clock says tickety-tock, now it's twelve
o'clock. It's noontime. "Do you want to stop
for lunch?" asks Mother.

We have hot dogs on rolls and ice-cold sodas.
I put on the mustard and ketchup by myself.

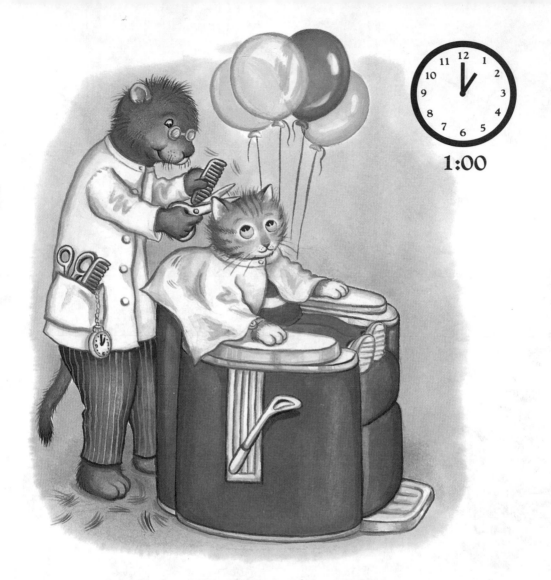

The clock says tickety-tock, now it's one o'clock in the afternoon. "It's time for your appointment with the barber," says Mother.

I sit in a big, tall chair. If I am very still while I get my hair cut, I can choose a big bright balloon to take home with me.

The clock says tickety-tock, now it's two o'clock. "Let's go to the department store next," says Mother.

I choose a new lunch box. Then I get a red-and-blue-checkered jacket and two pairs of corduroy pants. I even try on a new pair of jeans. Later we go downstairs to buy my notebook and a pencil case.

3:00

The clock says tickety-tock, now it's three
o'clock. "We have one more stop to make,"
says Mother.

It's the ice-cream shop! I have a big scoop of
black raspberry with hot fudge on top. Mother
has her favorite—chocolate chocolate chip.

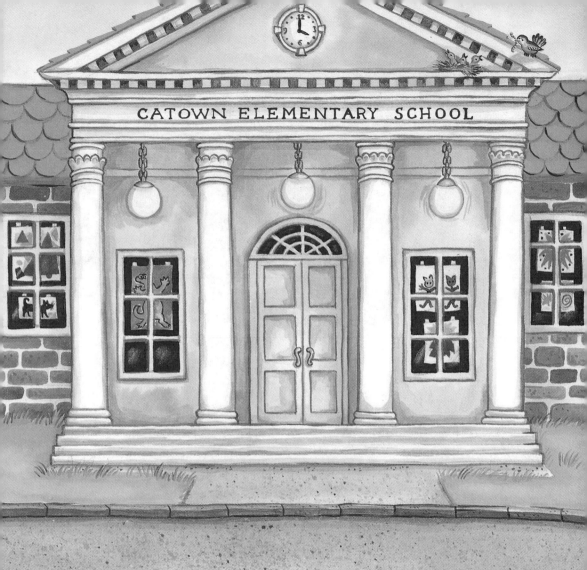

The clock says tickety-tock, now it's four
o'clock. "It's time to go home," says Mother.
   On the way home we drive by my school. I
see one of my drawings from last year in the
window.

5:00

Finish

The clock says tickety-tock, now it's five o'clock. "You can go and play while I make dinner," says Mother.

I'm off to the speedway in a flash! Today's the biggest race of the year, and my green car is going to win!

6:00

The clock says tickety-tock, now it's six
o'clock in the evening. "Dinner's ready," calls
Mother from the kitchen.

I have a chicken drumstick and a wing and
lots of potatoes. The salad tastes good with
dressing on top. "What did you do today?"
asks Father.

The clock says tickety-tock, now it's seven
o'clock. "Get ready for your bath," says Father.
Father always helps me with my bath. He
helps me wash behind my ears and all over
my face. But most of all he helps me sail my
toy boats.

8:00

The clock says tickety-tock, now it's eight
o'clock. "It's time for bed," calls Mother.
    Mother comes in to kiss me good night, but
Father stays to read me a story. I fall asleep
before he finishes. After all, tomorrow is the
first day of school, and I have to be up at...
tickety-tock, seven o'clock in the morning.